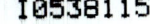

THE WHATS

What Is A What?

Written By: J.P. Freeman

Illustrated by: L.Kvirikashvili

For Wyatt,

I love you, sweet boy

A What is a What, so you shall see!

But what is a What and

what does it say?

A What is a What and
Whats love to play!

But Mr. What, it's the middle of the night.

A What pays no mind to the darkness or light.

Shhh! My parents are asleep
in the room right next door!

If they really were...they aren't anymore!

Please, Mr. What could you try to be quiet?

I probably could, but I'd be the first
What to try it!

But, what is a What and
from where do you come?

Neither here nor there is a
What's rule of thumb.

Whats have to belong somewhere.
Did you come from the zoo?

A What in a cage?! This just will not do!

When it comes to Whats,
I just don't know where to begin.

A What is a What! I'll say it again!

Please Mr. What, try to lower your voice!

Whats are loud, we don't have a choice!

I can hear my parents coming down the hall!

And when they arrive there will be no
Whats at all!

That was a What, playing with my toys.

But, what is a What and

what does it do?

A What is a What. Yes, a What through and through.

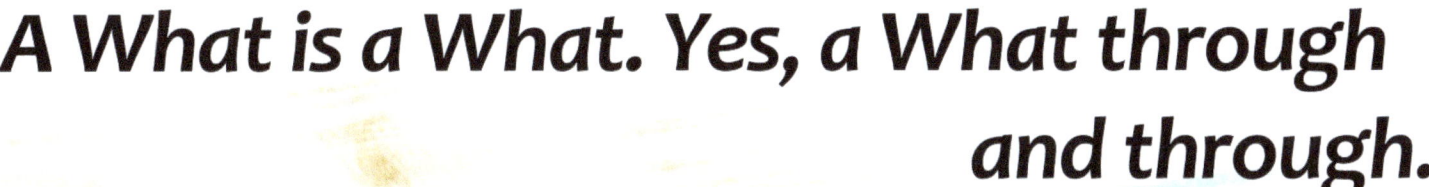